Dash's BellyAche

A BOOK FOR KIDS WHO WON'T POOP OR ARE AFRAID TO POOP.

Dash Learns Life Skills Series

Dedicated to my sons,
Zachary and Nathaniel

Dash's Belly Ache, written and illustrated by Wendy Hayden

SWH Medial LLC.

www.NaturalConstipationSolutions.com

Cover by Wendy Hayden

"Dash, would you like to go to the park?" asked Mama.
"Yes, Mama, I would love to go to the park!" said Dash.

Mama said, "Dash, you should try to go potty
before we go to the park!"

"No, Mama! I don't have to go potty.
I am ready to play!" said Dash.

"Are you sure?" asked Mama.
"Yes, Mama, I'm sure" said Dash.

But when Dash got to the park,
his tummy started to hurt.

And he couldn't play with his friends.

Mama said, "We need to go home if you aren't feeling well."

Dash thought the walk home felt very long
with his tummy hurting.

Dash was sad that he hadn't felt good
enough to play with his friends.

Mama asked, "Are you sure you don't have to go potty, Dash?"

"I'm sure, I don't have to go, Mama" said Dash.

"Won't you try for me?" asked Mama.

"I don't want to go potty, Mama!" exclaimed Dash.

Dash tried to eat his dinner
but his tummy felt too full to eat.

Mama was worried.

When Dash got in bed, his tummy really hurt.
He had a hard time falling asleep.

When Dash woke up the next morning, he felt even worse.

Dash couldn't eat his breakfast, either.

When Dash didn't feel like playing after breakfast,

Mama decided it was time to take Dash
to see Dr. Faniel.

Dash was nervous about going to the doctor's office.

Dr. Faniel asked, "Dash, what hurts?"

Dash said, "My tummy hurts."

After feeling Dash's tummy, Dr. Faniel asked,
"When was the last time you went poop?"

Dash said, "I can't remember but it has been a few days."

Dr. Faniel decided that Dash needed some special dog treats
that would help him to go potty.

Dash felt very relieved.
The doctor visit hadn't been scary at all!

Dash ate his special treats.

Dash's tummy was gurgling.

But it didn't feel bad.

It felt like he needed to go potty!

Dash ran outside.

And pooped!

Dash felt great!

His tummy didn't hurt anymore!

Dash slept great and woke up feeling AWESOME!

Dash was so excited to go back to the park and play with his friends!

Dash loved playing frisbee!

Dash had a great time playing with his friends.

Dash was so glad that his belly felt better!

Pooping is awesome!

If your child enjoyed this book, please leave a review!

Dash's Special Treat

For the recipe for Dash's Special Treat, please visit:

https://naturalconstipationsolutions.com/recipe/dashs-special-treat-poop-candy

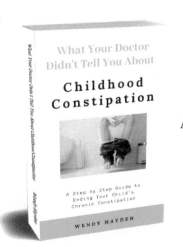

What Your Doctor Didn't Tell You About Childhood Constipation

A step-by-step guide that will help you to find a regiment that will help your child have 1-3 bowel movements a day and get to the root cause of their chronic constipation.

Also available by Wendy Hayden

Check out all of my resources I have to help you
including free constipation relief workbooks, a free
5 day Healthy Bathroom Habits challenge, books,
courses and so much more:
https://naturalconstipationsolutions.com/Resources